THE SAGA OF YNGVAR THE FAR-TRAVELLED

Odd Snorrason

THOR'S STONE PRESS

INTRODUCTION

It is the fantastic events narrated in this saga that have led to its inclusion in the legendary saga sub-genre, rather than its temporal setting. While most legendary sagas are set in a remote antiquity predating the dawn of the Viking Age, that of Yngvar the Far Traveller contains a fabulous account of the adventures of a historical Swede, attested not only in more reputable sagas and chronicles, but also in a series of Swedish runestones, memorials of men who sailed with the protagonist 'to Serkland (a vague geographical term suggesting the Islamic world)' and died during the journey.

The historical background is Sweden and Russia in the 1040s, very close to what historians regard as the close of the Viking Age. The last of several Viking expeditions to the Caspian was undertaken by Ingvar Vittfarne, to give the Swedish form of his name, in 1041, and evidence exists that he and his men were involved in a battle between the Georgians and Byzantine Greeks (the Battle of Sasireti) the following year. Other than this and the runestones, historical corroboration is scanty, and no consensus

1

exists as to Yngvar/Ingvar's precise identity, as is indeed stated by the author of this saga.

Odd Snorrason's authorship has been debated. Little is known of this twelfth century Benedictine monk, other than that he pursued his vocation at the Thingeyraklaustur monastery, except that he is believed to have written a Latin version of *The Saga of Olaf Tryggvason*. The latter is only preserved in *The Saga of Odd the Monk*, a fragmentary Old Norse translation, which was one of the sources drawn upon by Snorri Sturluson when he wrote his *Heimskringla,* and is a far cry from the wonders, marvels and monsters described in *The Saga of Yngvar.* The saga draws extensively upon medieval bestiaries and travel literature to create a saga as fantastic as any located in the legendary past.

CHAPTER ONE

Eirik was the name of a king who ruled over Sweden. He was called Eirik the Victorious. He married Sigrid the Proud, and divorced her because of her foul moods, for she was the most quarrelsome of women about all that happened to her. He gave her Gautland. Their son was Olaf the Swede.

At that time Earl Hakon ruled over Norway and had many children, and about one of his daughters we will say something, a woman named Aud. King Eirik also had a daughter, who is not named. A Swedish chief, whose name was Aki, asked for her hand, but the king seemed loath to marry his daughter to a common man. Shortly afterwards a petty king from east in Russia asked for her, and it seemed fitting to the king to marry the maiden to him, and she went with him east to Russia. Sometime later Aki came by surprise and killed the king but took the king's daughter away with him and went home to Sweden and married her. Eight chiefs plotted this with Aki and stayed there for a time under the king's rule, because the king would not fight with them or make so great a loss of men within his own land. Aki had a son who was named Eymund.

After this, Aki offered settlement to the king for this recklessness. The king took it well, and now when this had happened, King Eirik asked for the hand of Aud, daughter of Earl Hakon of Norway. This speech was favourably answered, but the earl, however, would have thought it better, if he had not let his son-in-law sit as high as he did in Sweden. Now the woman was promised, and the wedding settled, and now words were exchanged again between Aki and the king, and Aki told the king that he could set terms of any kind except outlawry, and he agreed to it. The king now made ready for his wedding, and invited the chiefs in the land, and the first he asked was Aki, his brother-in-law, and the eight chiefs who followed him.

CHAPTER TWO

On the day named Earl Hakon came from Norway to Sweden, and there was a great throng at Uppsala, because all the best men from Sweden were there. There were many large huts, for there were many chiefs come in large numbers, though Aki's was the biggest throng, barring King Eirik and Earl Hakon's following. So the hut that was second biggest was readied for Aki. Neither the king's daughter nor their son was there, for the king's summons seemed untrustworthy.

Now men sat at the feast for a while with great joy and merriment. At the start of the feast, Aki too much care for his own safety, but less as the wedding went on, until one night was left of the feast. Then King Eirik came there with them all unaware and killed all the eight chiefs who had been against the king, and also Aki. After that the feast ended. Earl Hakon went to Norway, and all others went to their own homes. Some men blame Earl Hakon for this plot, and some say that he was the one who killed them.

Now the king took ownership of all the lands and chattels that the eight chiefs had owned. He took

Eymund and his mother back home. Eymund grew up with the king in good standing, until King Eirik died. Then Olaf took the kingdom and kept Eymund in the same standing as his father had done.

But when Eymund was grown up, he remembered his sorrows, for every day he saw his belongings before his eyes, and he thought himself stripped of all honour, for the king took all the tribute from his belongings. King Olaf had a daughter named Ingigerd. Eymund and she loved each other greatly due to their kinship, and she was a good woman in every way. Eymund was a great man of growth and height and was the best knight.

Eymund now thought of his case, and thought recompense for his sorrows was coming slowly, and thought a quick death better than to live with shame. Now it came to his awareness that when he heard that twelve men of the king's court had gone after tribute to the shires and kingdoms which his father had owned, he went with twelve men to the woods which lay along their way, and they fought the king's men there, and there was a hard battle with them.

That same day Ingigerd went through those woods and found all dead but Eymund, and he was badly wounded. Then she had him laid in her wagon and carried him away and had him healed secretly. But when King Olaf heard of these tidings, he called the meeting, and proclaimed Eymund guilty and outlawed him from all his kingdom. And when Eymund was healed, Ingigerd gave him a ship in secret, and he went to war and did well for money and men.

CHAPTER THREE

Some winters later a king asked to marry Ingigerd, he was named Jarizleif, and he ruled over Russia. She was given to him, and she went east with him. But when Eymund heard the tidings, he went east then, and King Jarizleif welcomed him and Ingigerd, for then there was a great war in Russia, for Burizleif, King Jarizleif's brother, attacked the kingdom. With him Eymund had five battles, but in the last one Burizleif was taken prisoner and blinded and brought to the king. There he got much money in gold and silver and many kinds of riches and good things. Then Ingigerd sent men to meet King Olaf, her father, and asked him to give up the lands which Eymund had, and make peace, rather than that he should be always foreseeing his attack; and it could be said that that a settlement was gained. At that time Eymund was in Holmgard, and he often had battles, and had victory in all, and won much tribute from the king. Then Eymund wished to visit his lands, and had a large and well-equipped force, for there was no lack of money or weapons.

Now Eymund left the kingdom of Gardar with great honour and esteem from all the folk, and now he came to Sweden and settled in his land and property, and soon he took to wife a powerful man's daughter, and he got a son with her who was named Yngvar.

It reached Olaf, king of Sweden, that Eymund had come ashore with a big troop and enough money and had settled in the kingdom which his father and the eight chiefs had, and he thought much about it, but did not trust himself to do anything, because every day he heard many great deeds of Eymund spoken about. And now each one sat quietly, for neither wanted to bow to the other.

Eymund now sat in his kingdom, ordered and ruled it as kings are wont, and broadened his kingdom, for he came to rule many. He had a great hall built, and lived well, and he kept a table there every day with a large throng, because he had many knights and enough ships. He now sat quietly.

Yngvar now grows up at home with his father, until he was nine years old. Then Yngvar asked his father if he could go to meet the king and other chiefs in Sweden. He let him go and made ready his journey with honour. Yngvar took his father's helmet, which was the best he had, - it was red golden and set with precious stones - and a sword inlaid with gold, and he had many other treasures. Yngvar now went with fourteen men from his father, and all their horses were armoured, and so were they themselves, and they had shield, and had golden helmets, and all weapons made of gold and silver. And with such an organised force he went west through Sweden. Many now heard about his journey, and the chiefs came to meet him in many places and invited him to a feast. He accepts it, and they give him good gifts, and he gives them much.

Now Yngvar's fame spread far and wide over Sweden and came to the ears of King Olaf. He had a son named Onund, and he was the most promising person, and not far from Yngvar in age. He asked his father to go to meet Yngvar, his nephew, and greet him with honour, and then he did as he asked, and went to meet Yngvar with great honour, and there was much rejoicing. Then they went to meet the king, and he went to meet them, and greeted them fittingly, and Yngvar, and led him into his hall, and welcomed him and all his company. He said he would stay there for a while.

Then he carried out the treasures that had been mentioned before, the helmet and the sword, and said thus: "These gifts my father sent you to strengthen peace and affirm friendship."

The king thankfully accepted the treasures but said that Eymund had not sent them for him. Yngvar was there all winter and was most respected by all the men of the king. In the spring Yngvar made ready to go home, and Onund with him. Then the king gave Yngvar a good horse and a golden saddle and a beautiful ship.

Now Yngvar and Onund went away in good favour from King Olaf, and then came to Eymund. And when they came to Eymund's house, he was told who had come, but he let it seem he had not heard. Now they came to the hall, and Onund wanted to dismount, but Yngvar told them ride into the hall. They did so, riding all the way inside to Eymund's throne. He greeted them fittingly and asked their tidings, and why they dared to go so far as to ride into his hall.

Then answered Yngvar: "When I came to King Olaf, he went to meet me with all his court and greeted me well and honourably, but you would not do any honour to his son when he seeks you at home. Now you know that for this I rode into your hall."

Then Eymund sprang up, and helped Onund off the horse and kissed him and sat him down, and said that all within the hall should serve him. Then Yngvar brought the gifts to his father, which he said King Olaf had sent him for lasting peace. It was the horse, the saddle, and the ship. Then Eymund said that King Olaf had not sent them for him, but he praised him much because he had given such worthy gifts to Yngvar. Onund was there that winter.

In the spring he made ready to go home, and Yngvar with him. Then Eymund gave Onund a hawk with a golden hue to its feathers, and they went away with this gift, and came to meet King Olaf, and he greeted

11

them fittingly, and was glad of their return. Then Onund brought him the hawk and said that Eymund had sent it to him.

Then the king reddened and said that Eymund could have named him when he gave the hawk, "but still it may be that he thought of us."

Some time later he called Onund and Yngvar to him and said, "Now you shall go and bring to Eymund what I would give him; and that is a banner, for I have no other wonderful gifts to give him like this. It follows that the one who bears it in the fight will always have victory, and this shall be a sign of settlement between us."

Now they went back and gave Eymund the banner with the king's friendly words. Eymund thankfully took the king's gift and said that he would soon go and invite King Olaf to him, and say thus: "Eymund, your servant, invites you to a feast with kindness, and I'll be grateful if you go."

They went and found King Olaf and gave him Eymund's invitation. Then King Olaf was very glad and went with a great throng. Eymund received him well, and with great honour, and they spoke of firm friendship with each other, and kept it well.

Then the king went home with good gifts, and Yngvar was always with the king, because he loved him no less than his son. Yngvar was a tall man, handsome and strong and fair of face, wise and well-spoken, mild and open handed with his friends, but grim with his enemies, courteous and quick in all his dealings, so wise men have always likened him to Styrbjorn, his nephew, or King Olaf Tryggvason, who was the most renowned man and will be in the Northern lands for ages and ages, before God and men.

CHAPTER FOUR

When the kinsmen, Onund and Yngvar, were full-grown, King Olaf was at odds with the nation called Semigallia, who had not paid tribute for a while. Then King Olaf sent Onund and Yngvar with three ships to gather tribute. They came ashore and arranged a meeting with the men of the land, and there demanded tribute from their king. Yngvar showed great skill in his speech, until the king and many other chiefs seemed to have no choice but to pay the tribute called, barring three chiefs, who did not want to follow the king's counsel and refused to pay the tribute and mustered their troops. But when the king heard of their plans, he told Onund and Yngvar to fight against them, and gave them help. They fought, and there was a great loss of life before the chiefs fled. In that flight the man who had been most against the tribute was taken, and they hanged him, but the other two got away. There they took much wealth as booty, and so gathered all the tribute, and went to meet King Olaf, and gave him a large sum of money in gold and silver and good treasures, and Yngvar's honour was greatly enlarged in this voyage, so that the king set him above the other chiefs of Sweden. Yngvar took a mistress and she gave birth to a son named Svein.

Yngvar was in favour with King Olaf until he was twenty. Then he grew unhappy, so that he never uttered a word. The king thought it a great shame and asked what the matter was.

Yngvar answered: "If you think it's a shame that I'm unhappy, and you wish me as well as you can, then give me the name of king with all dignity."

The king answered, "I will do every other thing that you ask for, regarding honour or wealth. But I cannot do this, for I am no wiser than my forefathers, and I know no better than our former kinsmen."

This matter put them at odds, because Yngvar always asked for name of king but did not get it.

CHAPTER FIVE

Then Yngvar made ready to leave the land to seek a far-off kingdom and chose a troop from the country and thirty ships, all fully equipped. Now when King Olaf heard that Yngvar was ready to go, he sent men to meet Yngvar and asked him to stay and take the name of king. Yngvar said that he would have taken it if it had been offered before but said that he had now to sail when the wind blew.

A little afterwards Yngvar sailed from Sweden with thirty ships and did not stop sailing until they came to Russia, and King Jarizleif received him with great honour. Yngvar was there three winters and he learned many tongues there. He heard a debate about the three rivers that flowed out of the east in Russia, and the middle one was the largest. Then Yngvar went far and wide through the eastern kingdom, and asked if any man knew where it flowed from, but no one could tell him.

Then Yngvar made ready his journey from Russia and he intended to try and learn the length of this river. He had the bishop hallow his flint and wood-axe. Four men are named with Yngvar on the journey: Hjalmvíg and Soti, Ketil, who was called

Garda-Ketil, he was an Icelander, and Valdimar. After that they sailed down the river with thirty ships, and Yngvar turned his prows to the east, and made sure that no one should go ashore without his leave. But if any man went overboard, then he should lose his hand or his foot. A man should stay awake at night on every ship.

When they had gone for a while along the river, it is said that Ketil had a watch to keep one night, and he thought it long that all the folk slept, and he was curious to go ashore to look around and he went farther than he meant to. He stopped and listened. He saw a house in front of him, very high, and he went there and entered the house, and there he saw a silver cauldron over a fire and thought it strange. He took the cauldron and ran to the ships. And when he had been going for a while, he saw at his back an awful giant running after him. Ketil then hastened his journey, and yet it drew closer. He set down the cauldron and took off the handle and ran as fast as he could, but sometimes he looked back. He saw that the giant stopped when he came to the cauldron. He sometimes went to it, but sometimes away, but at last picked up the cauldron and went home, but Garda-Ketil went to the ships and broke up the handle and put it in his foot-chest.

But in the morning, when the men awoke and went ashore, they saw a trail running from the ships, because dew had fallen, and they told Yngvar. He asked Ketil to say if he had gone there, because he could name no one else, and said he would not kill him if he told the truth. He said he had and asked for mercy for his unruliness and showed him the handle. Yngvar told him not to do this again, and he agreed.

Then they sailed for many days and through many places, and until they saw other ways of life and beasts of different hues, and from that they understood that they were moving away from their own lifestyles and lands. One evening they saw from afar what looked like a half-moon standing on the earth. The next night Valdimar kept watch. He went ashore in search of the place where they had seen this. He came to the place where there was a hill rising that seemed to be coloured gold, and he saw what caused it, because everything there was covered with snakes. But as they slept, he stretched out his spear to a gold ring, and drew it to himself. Then one of the snakes awoke, and he at once woke the others by him, until Jaculus[1] was awake. Then Valdimar hurried to the ships and told Yngvar all the truth. Now Yngvar told the men to wait for the snake and steer the ships to another harbour across the river, and so they did. Then they saw a dreadful dragon flying over the river. Many hid for fear. And when Jaculus came across a ship that two priests steered, he spewed so much poison that both ships and men were lost. Then he flew across the river to his lair.

Then Yngvar went many days along the river. Then

towns and large settlements appeared, and then they saw a worthy town. It was made of white marble. And as they approached the town, they saw many women and men. They thought much of the fairness of those who were there, and the courtesy of women, for many were beautiful to see. However, one of them stood out from the others for the sake of both her clothes and her beauty. The worthy woman signalled to Yngvar, that they should meet her. Then Yngvar got off the ship and met that lovely woman. She asked who they were or what they did, but Yngvar did not answer, for he wanted to test if she could speak more tongues; and so it turned out that she could speak Latin, German, Danish and Russian and many others spoken in the East.

But when Yngvar heard these tongues from her, he told her his name and asked her name and what rank she had.

"My name is Silkisif," she said, "and I am the queen of this land and kingdom."

Then she asked Yngvar to come to the town with her, and all his men. He agreed. And the townsfolk took their ships with all their rigging and carried them up before the town. Yngvar readied a hall for all his troop, and locked it carefully, because it was full of blood sacrifices all around. Yngvar told them beware of the fellowship of the heathen, and he banned all women from coming to his hall other than the queen. Some men paid little heed to his words, and he had them killed, and then no one dared to break what he ordered.

That winter Yngvar was there in good spirits, because the queen sat every day talking with him and her sages, and they told each other many tidings. Yngvar often told her of the Almighty God, and the faith interested her. She loved Yngvar so much that she invited him to take the whole kingdom and the name of king, and she gave herself in to his power, if he wished to stay there, but he said he would first explore the length of the river and take that choice afterwards.

When spring came, Yngvar got ready to go, and asked the queen to stay with her folk. Yngvar went up the river until he came to a great waterfall and a narrow gorge. There were high cliffs, so that they pulled up their ships. Then they dragged them back to the river and it went so long that they did not see much. But as the summer wore on, they saw several ships rowing towards them. They were all round and had oars on every side. They set out in such a way that Yngvar had no choice but to wait, for their ships went as fast as a bird flies. But before they could meet, one of the men rose up from the troop. He was adorned with a king's finery and spoke many tongues. Yngvar was quiet. Then he spoke a few words of Russian. Yngvar understood that his name was Jolf, and he was from the town of Heliopolis[2]. And when the king knew Yngvar's name, and where he had come from, or where he meant to go, he invited him to stay in his town over the winter. Yngvar did not want to stay and refused. The king then demanded he stay there that winter. Yngvar said he should do so. Then they went with their troop to the harbour and went ashore and to the town. And they were astonished when they saw that the townsfolk carried their ships on their shoulders up under the town, where it was possible to lock them up. There they saw in all the streets many sacrifices. Yngvar told his men be devout and faithful. Jolf gave them a hall, and that winter Yngvar kept his men in such a way that no one was harmed by women's lures or other heathen nonsense. But when they went to carry out their business, they went fully armed and locked the hall in the meantime. No man should go in there but the king. Every day he sat talking to Yngvar, and each told the other many tidings from his country, new or old.

Yngvar asked if he knew where the river rose, and Jolf said he knew it to be true that it rose from the spring, "which we call Lindibelt. Another flows from there to the Red Sea[3], and there is a great whirlpool, the one called Gapi. Between the sea and the river is a headland called Siggeum. The river flows a little way before it falls from a cliff into the Red Sea, and we call it the end of the world. And upon the river you are following, scoundrels lie out in large ships, and all the ships are covered up by reeds, so that men think them islands, and they have all kinds of weapons and flame siphons[4], and they destroy men more with fire than with weapons."

But the townsfolk thought that their king did not do what they needed regarding Yngvar, and they offered to drive him from the kingdom, and take another king. And when Yngvar heard this, he told the king do the will of his folk. He did so. The king asked Yngvar to help him fight his brother. He was the strongest of them and gave much trouble to his brother. Yngvar vowed to help when he came back.

CHAPTER SIX

At the end of the winter, Yngvar led his whole host out of Jolf's kingdom. And when they had gone for a while, they came to a great waterfall. From it came such a great spray that they had to land. And when they came ashore, they saw the footprints of an awful giant. It was eight feet long. There were such high rocks that they could not pull the ships up with cables. They set out along the cliffs on their ships, from where the river and the current curved. There was a small gap in the cliffs, and they went ashore there, and it was flat and wet. Yngvar told them to cut down trees and make digging tools, and so they did; then began to dig, and measured a deep and wide dike into which the river was to flow. They were at this for months before they could sail that way.

And when they had been going a long time, they saw a house and a terrible giant so ugly that they thought it was the devil. They were very frightened and asked God for mercy. Then Yngvar asked Hjalmvigi to sing psalms to the glory of God, for he was a good priest, and they swore they would spend six days of fasting with prayer. Then the giant walked away from the house down the way by the river. And when he was gone, they went to the house and saw an earthwork there. And when they went into the house, they saw that one of the pillars held it up; it was made of clay. Then they began to cut the pillar all around the base, until the house shook when they cut. Yngvar then told them take large stones and carry them to the house. They did so. But when twilight fell, Yngvar told them go to the earthwork and hide in the reeds. And in the evening, they saw the giant coming, and he had many men fastened under his belt. He carefully locked up the fort and also the house. Then he ate. But as time passed, they wondered what he was doing, and heard a great snore. Then Yngvar told them take away the stones which they had carried there, and threw them at the pillar, so that the house fell down. The giant struggled violently, so that he got one of his legs free. Then Yngvar and his companions went and cut off the giant's leg with axes, for he was as hard as a tree. And when it was over, they understood that he was dead. They dragged the feet to the ship and salted it in white salt.

They now went until the river split, and they saw five islands stirring and going towards them. Yngvar told his men to expect attack. He lit a fire with the blessed flint. Soon an island came to them and threw stones at them, but they protected themselves and shot back. But when the vikings[5] saw what faced them, they began to blow blacksmiths' bellows into the furnace in which there was a fire, and a great rumble ensued. There was also a bronze siphon, and from it a great fire poured onto a ship, and it burned in a short time, so that everything became ashes. But when Yngvar saw that, he mourned his loss, and told him bring the tinder with the blessed fire. Then he pointed his bow upwards and put an arrow on a string and had the tinder with the blessed fire placed on the arrowhead. And the arrow flew from the bow with the fire into the siphon which stood out of the furnace, and the fire turned on the heathen themselves, and in a brief while the island burned with everything, men and ships. And the other islands have arrived. And when Yngvar heard the sound of a bellows, he fired a blessed fire, and so destroyed the devil's folk with God's help, so that it became nothing but ashes.

A little after, Yngvar came to the source from which the river rose. There they saw a dragon of a kind that had never been seen before for the sake of its size, and much gold lay beneath it. They landed a short way from there, and all went ashore, and came to the place where the dragon was used to crawl into the water. That pathway was very wide. Then Yngvar told them to sow salt along the path and drag the giant's foot there, and he said that he thought that the dragon would halt there for a while. They kept quiet and took cover. But when the time came that the dragon was accustomed to crawl to the water, and he came to the path, he saw that there was salt in the pathway in front of him, and he began to lick. And when he came to the place where the giant's foot lay, he straightaway swallowed it. He was now longer on the path he usually followed, for three times he turned back to drink, by the time he was in the middle. But Yngvar and his followers went to the dragon's lair and saw there much gold, and it was so hot as if it had just been melted in a forge. Then they cut off lumps with axes, and it was a great deal of money that they got there. They saw that the dragon was approaching. They went away with much money and hid it. Many reeds grew there. Yngvar told them to ignore the dragon. They did as he commanded, but a few men stood up and saw that the dragon was angry at its loss. He lifted his tail and sounded like a man whistling and turned in a circle on the gold. They told the others what things they had seen, and then fell down dead.

CHAPTER SEVEN

After this event Yngvar and his men went away and explored the headland that they had come to. There they found a castle and saw a large hall standing there. And when they came into the hall, they saw it was well furnished inside, and there they found a great treasure and many riches. Then Yngvar asked if anyone would stay there the night and see what tidings he might learn. Soti said it would be no trouble. And when twilight fell, Yngvar went with his group to the ships, but Soti hid somewhere.

And when it was late, he saw the devil come in man's shape, and he said, "There was a man named Siggeus, strong and mighty. He had three daughters. He gave them much gold. But when he died, he was buried there, where you now saw the dragon. After he died the eldest begrudged her sisters getting gold and jewels. She killed herself. Her second sister followed her example. The third sister lived longest and she took her father's heirlooms and wardenship of the place, and not only while she was still alive. She named this headland and called it Siggeum. She fills the hall every night with several devils, and I am one of them, sent to tell you these tidings. But dragons devoured the king's corpse and the bodies of his daughters. Some think they have become dragons. Know this, Soti, and tell your king, Yngvar, that King Harald[6] of Sweden went this way a long time ago, and he was swallowed up by the Red Sea with his following, and he is now here as the warden. And to prove what I say is true, the banner of King Harald is kept in the hall, and Yngvar shall have it and send it to Sweden, so that they may know what had become of their king. Tell Yngvar that he will die in this journey with a large part of his host. But you, Soti, are unjust and unbelieving, so stay with us; but Yngvar will be helped by the faith he has in God."

Then the devil who had said this fell silent. All night there was a great and loud din. And in the morning Yngvar came and Soti told him about what he had seen and heard, and when Soti had finished his story, he fell down dead in front of all the onlookers.

Now Yngvar took the banner which stood in the hall, and then went to his ships with his host. He now turned his prows and gave a name for the great waterfall and called it Belgsoti[7]. Then nothing is said of their journey until they came into the kingdom of King Hromund, whose name was Jolf.

And when they sailed for the second time to the town of Heliopolis, King Jolf sent out against them many ships, and told Yngvar lower his sails, "for now you shall give me a host to fight against Bjolf, my brother, who is called Solmund by another name, for he himself and his eight sons want to rob me of the kingdom."

Then Yngvar went to the town and made ready for battle. Yngvar had large wheels built and fixed around with sharp points and spikes; he also had caltrops made.

Now both kings gather their troops and come to the place that they had decided on among themselves. And when Yngvar had form up his ranks, Bjolf's forces were much more plentiful. King Jolf ranked his host against his brother. And when they were both done, they shouted a war cry. Yngvar and his men pushed those wheels with all their armour, and a great loss of life followed, and the host was torn to shreds. Then Yngvar came to them in the open, and killed all the sons of King Bjolf, but he himself fled.

King Jolf pursued fiercely and chased the run-aways, but Yngvar told his men to stay behind and not go too far from their ships - "because our enemies may take them. It would be better to take much plunder from the bodies of our dead foes."

There they took many kinds of treasures and a large sum of money and carried them to the ships. Then Jolf came with the host, and mustered his ranks, and gave a war-cry, but Yngvar was surprised, and commanded a retreat. Then he cast caltrops under their feet. They could not avoid them and ran onto them. And when they learnt the sharpness of the spikes, they thought they had met with witchcraft. But Yngvar was back at the camp, and there they plundered the treasures. Then they saw a large group of women walking to the camp, and they began to play music beautifully. Yngvar then told them to beware the women as if they were the worst venomous worms. And when the evening took hold and the host got ready to go to bed, the women went to their camp, but the one who was most stately got into bed with Yngvar. Then he grew angry, took a knife, and thrust it into the woman's cunt. And when his men saw his deed, they began to drive away these lewd women, and yet there were some of them who could not stand up to the tenderness of the devil's charms and lay with them. But when Yngvar heard this, his rejoicing at silver and the joy of wine turned into great sorrow, for in the morning eighteen men lay dead when he surveyed their host. Then Yngvar asked for those who were dead to be buried.

CHAPTER EIGHT

And after this Yngvar left in haste with all his men, and now they went on their way and now went day and night, as fast as they could. But such a sickness began to grow in the host that all their best folk died, and a greater part fell than lived. Yngvar also took sick, and by then they had come to the kingdom of Silkisif. He then called his host to him and asked them to bury those who were dead.

Then he called to him Garda-Ketil and his other friends, and said, "I have taken sick, and I see that it will lead me to death, and then I will have the place which I have won. And with God's mercy I hope that the Son of God will grant me his vow, for with all my heart I entrust myself to the hands of God every day, my soul and body, and I will take care of this folk as best I can. But I want you to know that that by the right judgment of God are we struck by this plague, and it is the worst of all plagues and bewitchment that has struck me, for when I am dead, the plague will go. And I ask of you, and most of all Ketil, that you bring my body to Sweden and bury it in a church. But my treasure that I have of gold and silver and rich clothing I want split into thirds: one third for the churches and priests, another for poor men, while my father and my son shall have a third. Bring Queen Silkisif my greetings! And for all things I want to pray that you are at peace with each other. But if you debate what way to go, let Garda-Ketil decide, for he is the one with the best memory of you."

Then he told them to live well and meet in joy on the day of resurrection. He was spoken well of in many ways, and then lived a few days.

They carefully made ready his body and laid it in a coffin and then turned on their way and landed at the town of Citopolis. And it came to pass, when the queen knew their ships, that she went out to meet them with great honour. And when she saw them come ashore, she was unhappy, and it seemed to her that much had happened, and she could not see him she cared for more than anyone else. She then asked for tidings and in earnest of events about Yngvar's death and where they had left his body. They said he had been buried in the ground. She told them it was a lie and said she would have them killed if they did not tell the truth. Then they told her what provision Yngvar had made with them to dispose of his body and belongings. Then they gave her Yngvar's body. She had him carried to the town with great honour and made ready with wonderful balms for burial.

Then the queen told them go in the peace of God and Yngvar. "Your god is mine. Greet Yngvar's kin, when you come to Sweden, and ask some of them to come here with the teachers and christen this folk, and then a church will be built here, where Yngvar will rest."

And when Yngvar died, one thousand and forty and one winters had passed since the birth of Jesus Christ[8], and he was in his mid-thirties when he died, eleven winters after the fall of King Olaf Haraldsson the Saint[9].

Ketil and his men got ready to leave and told the queen to live well, and now they turned on their way and had twelve ships. And when they had gone for a while, they quarrelled about the way, and they parted, with no one wanting to follow another. But Ketil had the right course and came to Russia, but Valdimar came alone to Miklagard[10]. And we do not know for sure where the other ships ended up, for most folk are thought to have died, and we cannot say any more about Yngvar. But still we know that he did many great deeds in this journey, of which wise men have much to tell.

Ketil, of whom we said, was in the kingdom of Russia over the winter, and afterwards went to Sweden in the summer, and told the tidings of what had taken place in their journey and brought there the belongings of Yngvar to his son, whose name was Svein, and greeted him with the queen's message. Svein was at a young age and was of great height. He was a strong man and like his father. He went to war because he wanted to test himself first. And when some winters had passed, he came with a large force to Russia in the east and stayed there for the winter.

CHAPTER NINE

It is said that that winter Svein went to school, that he learned to speak many tongues, which men knew were used in the East. Then he made ready thirty ships and said he would take that host to meet the queen. He had many priests with him. The keenest was a bishop named Rodgeirr. The bishop blessed lots three times and cast three times, and each time they fell to say that God wanted him to go. The bishop then said he was glad to go.

Now Svein readied his journey to Russia. And when they had gone two days up the river, the heathen came upon them with ninety ships; of the kind the Norwegians call galleys. The heathens straightaway made ready for battle and so did the Swedes, but neither understood what the others said. But while they were donning their armour, Svein put his fate in God's hands, and cast lots to know whether it was God's will that they should come or flee with such great force. But the lot commanded them to fight, and Svein promised to give up war, if God would give him victory then. After this they began to fight, and Svein and his men killed the heathen as they wished, and in the end the heathens fled on twenty ships, but everyone else was killed, and Svein suffered little loss of life, but gained as much money as they wanted in gold and all kinds of treasure.

Then they went on their way, until they came to the land where Ketil had got the handle. Then Svein told most of his host put on armour, and so they did. And for a short time they went, before they saw a large town and a large man there, and he called out in a terrible voice. Then troops appeared from all over. Such folk are called Cyclopes. They had big clubs in their hands, like axes. They clustered together and had neither shields nor weapons.

Then Svein asked that the bowmen should shoot at them as quickly as possible, and said that they were not to wait around, "for they are as strong as the fearless beast[11], and as tall as houses or trees."

Then they shot at them and killed many, and wounded others. Then a wonderful thing happened, because then those who could have fought more fled. Svein banned his men from running after them and said they would have no cover. Then they ran to the settlement and plundered there much wealth in skins and clothes and silver and all costly metals, and now went to the ships and turned on their way.

When they had gone a long time, Svein saw where a creek cut into the land. He told them to steer the ships there. They were willing to do this, because there were many young men among them. And as they neared land, they saw castles and many settlements. Eight men they saw running and they wondered at their speed. One of the men of the land had a feather in his hand and held up a feather-adorned staff and then the feather itself. That seemed to them a sign of peace. Then Svein made a sign of peace with his hand. Then they landed, but the men of the land flocked together under a rock with many trade goods. Svein told his men to go ashore, and they and the men of the land traded, and yet they did not understand what the others were saying.

On the second day Svein's men again went to buy from the men of the land, and traded for a while. Then a Greek man wanted to go back on a deal over skins, that they had newly bought. Then the heathen became angry and hit him on the nose, so that blood sprang to the ground. Then the Greek drew his sword and cut the heathen in two. Then the men of the land ran away with a great scream and shout, and then a great host came. Then Svein told his men to armour themselves and march against them, and a hard and fierce battle between them followed, and many heathens fell, for they were all shieldless. But when they saw themselves overwhelmed, they fled, and there Svein took much wealth, which the others had left behind, and carried it to the ships.

But after this incident Svein went away from there and praised God for his victory. They went on for a while, until they saw a large herd of pigs on a headland under a cliff by the river, and some men ran ashore and wanted to kill them, and so they did. Then the pigs who had escaped began to squeal loudly and ran up onto the land. And then they saw a great host coming down from the land to the ships, and one man went somewhat ahead of the troop. He had three apples and threw one up in the air, and it came down at Svein's feet, and straight after another; it came down in the same place.

Then Svein said he would not wait for the third apple: "This comes from devilish power and strong belief."

Svein put an arrow to his string and shot at him. The arrow hit his nose. The noise was most like horn bursting asunder, and he turned his head, and they saw that he had a bird's nose. Then he shouted loudly, and ran to back his host, and so every one of them went inland who could, as long as they could see.

CHAPTER TEN

After that Svein returned to his ships, and now went on his way. And when they had been gone a short time, it is said that they saw during the day that ten men were leading after them some kind of living thing. They thought it was rather odd, for they saw a large tower of wood made standing behind the beast. Fifty men went ashore, who were most curious about the nature of the beast. But when those leading the beast saw the crew, they hid and unleashed the beast. But Svein's men went to the beast and wanted to lead it after them, but it put its head down, so that it did not move, though they all took to pulling the ropes that were on the beast's head. Then they thought that it was a trick they did not understand, that ten of them could lead the beast. Then they sought counsel, and went away from the beast, and hid in the reeds, so that they could learn all they could about the beast. And a little later the men of the land rose up and went to the beast. They took the ropes and put two of them either side of the neck, and then through a hole in a crosstree which stood on the tower, and so pulled up the head of the beast, for there was a pulley in the hole. But when Svein's men saw the beast standing upright, they ran there as fast as they could. They took them and led the beast where they wanted. But since they did not know the nature of the beast and what it needed for food, they thrust their spears into the beast, so that it fell down dead. Then they went down to the ships and rowed away.

And then they saw many heathens ashore, who went down to the shore and made Svein a sign of peace, and they straightaway landed the ships. There was a good harbour. And now they had a market between them, and Svein bought many treasures there. Then the heathen invited their merchants to a house for a feast, and they did so. And when they came to the house, they saw all kinds of dainties set out and enough of the best drinks. And when Svein's men sat down at the table, they crossed themselves; but when the heathen saw them making the sign of the cross, they became angry and rushed at them. Some beat them with their fists, and others egged them on, and both sides called for others to join them.

And when Svein heard the call of his men and saw their business, he said, "Who knows what has happened, unless the feast has turned into a great mishap?"

Then he went after them and told all his men to armour themselves. And when Svein had arrayed his host, they also saw where the heathens had arrayed their host, and that they carried a bloody man before the host and had him as a standard. Then Svein consulted with Bishop Rodgeir about what to do.

The bishop said, "If the heathens expect victory from the likeness of a wicked man, let us ponder that we are to expect the help of heaven, where the Lord Christ himself lives and is merciful; let us see the token of victory of Christ crucified before the host and call on His name, and from that we can expect victory, but the heathens to die."

After the bishop had egged them on, they took the holy cross with the likeness of the Lord and had it for a banner and carried it before the men. Then they fearlessly went to meet the heathens, while the learned men began to pray. And when the armies met together, the heathen became blind and many were terrified, and soon fled, and each ran his own way, some into the river, and some into the swamps or woods. Many thousands of heathens died there.

But when the run-aways were driven out, Svein had the bodies of those who had fallen there buried; but when this was done, Svein told his troop to beware of being curious about the customs of the heathen, "because there has been more," he said, "loss of life in this journey than profit."

CHAPTER ELEVEN

Then Svein went on, until it seemed to them that half a moon stood in the earth. There they landed and went ashore. Then Ketil told Svein the tidings of what had happened when Yngvar and his men were there. Then Svein asked his troop from the ships to hurry to meet the dragon. Then they went on and came to a large wood, which stood by the dragon's den, and hid there. Then Svein sent some young men to the dragon to learn what was going on there. They saw that the snakes were asleep, and there were many of them. However, Jaculus lay in a ring around all the others. Then one of them began to reach in with his spear-shaft for a gold ring, and the spear-shaft touched a little snake. And when it awoke, it awoke another, and then they awoke one by one, until Jaculus arose. Svein stood by a large oak and set an arrow to his string, and tinder was placed on the arrowhead as big as a human head with blessed fire. And when Svein saw that Jaculus was rising into the air and he was making for their ship and flew with gaping mouth, Svein shot the arrow with the blessed fire into the mouth of the worm, and it ran so close to his heart that in an instant he fell dead. And when Svein and his men saw it, they praised God with joy.

CHAPTER
TWELVE

After this event Svein told them to hurry away from the stench and reek that came from it. Then they went quickly to the ships, and most of them did so apart from six men, who went to look at the dragon out of curiosity, and they fell down dead. However, many folk were still very troubled by the reek, even though no more were killed.

Then Svein got ready quickly to leave there and went on, until he came to the kingdom of Queen Silkisif. She greeted them with great honour. And when Svein and his men got off the ships, Ketil went first to meet the queen, but she did not pay heed to him and turned to Svein and wanted to kiss him, but he dodged away from her and said he did not want to kiss her, a heathen woman, "and why do you want to kiss me?"

She answered: "Because you alone have Yngvar's eyes, as far as it seems to me."

Then they were welcome with honour and respect. And when she knew that the bishop had come there, she was glad. Then the bishop preached the faith to her, and they had an interpreter between them, because the bishop could not speak the tongue she spoke, and she soon gained an understanding of spiritual wisdom and was baptized. And in that same month all the folk of the town were baptized.

Not much later, the Queen called a general meeting of her folk. And when a great throng had gathered there, Svein Yngvarsson was decked with purple, and then a crown was set on his head, and all called him their king; and with that the queen married him.

CHAPTER
THIRTEEN

After the wedding feast King Svein went about his kingdom with a throng and so did the queen. There was also the bishop on the journey and learned men, for King Svein made the land Christian and all the kingdoms that the queen had formerly ruled. And when summer came, and so the power of divine mercy had manifested in that land, so it had become all Christian, King Svein and his followers wanted to make ready their journey home to Sweden and let their kin know the truth about his journey. But when the queen became aware of this plan, she asked him to send them home, but he should stay there himself.

Svein answered: "I do not want to send my troop away from me, for there is much hazard for them in many ways if they embark on this journey, as it turned out before, when no one was leader and the whole host died or got lost in many ways."

But when the queen heard the words of the king, and saw what he wanted to do, she said, "Do not go so suddenly, if I may say so, for it may be that you do not want to visit this kingdom again, or you could get lost on such a great hazardous journey as you tell me, what would be better is for you to strengthen Christianity and have churches built, for first you must have a church built within the town, great and venerable, and if it turns out as I wish, then we shall bury the body of your father there. But after three winters, go in peace."

Now it was done as the queen asked, that King Svein stayed there three winters. But in the third winter the great church in the town was finished. Then the queen asked the bishop to come.

But when the bishop was decked in his robes, he asked, "In what name, queen, do you want to bless the church?"

She answers. "In honour of King Yngvar, who rests here, shall this church be blessed."

The bishop answered: "Why do you want that, queen? Or has Yngvar worked miracles on the earth after his death? Because we call only men saints if a miracle occurs when their bodies are buried in the ground."

She answers: "From your mouth I hear that there is more worth to God in confirming the true faith and the habit of holy love than the glory of miracles; but I judge, as I saw, that Yngvar was steadfast in holy love for God."

When the queen said that it should be so, the bishop blessed the temple to the glory of God and to all the saints by the name of Yngvar. Then a new stone coffin was hewn and Yngvar's body set within and over it was set a cross with splendid ornamentations. Then the bishop had Mass sung in public for Yngvar's soul, and even allowed the folk to call it Yngvar's Church.

CHAPTER FOURTEEN

When these things were done Svein made ready to leave and he went north until he came to Sweden. The folk of the land received him with joy and great honour. He was offered the land[12]. But when he heard that, he quickly refused and said that he had gained a better and happier land, and that he would return to it.

And when two winters were out, Svein sailed from Sweden, but Ketil stayed behind, and he was told that Svein was in Russia during the winter and made ready to depart from there in the spring and sailed from Russia in the summer, and folk knew that the last time he was seen, he was sailing down the river.

But Ketil went to Iceland to meet his kinsmen and settled there, and was the first to tell of this, but we know that some storytellers say that Yngvar was the son of Eymund Olafsson, for they think it more praiseworthy to say he was the king's son. But Onund would gladly have given up all his kingdom, if he could buy back Yngvar's life, for all the chiefs in Sweden would gladly have had him king over him. But some folk still ask why Yngvar was not the son of Eymund Olafsson, and we will answer this way: Eymund, son of Olaf, had a son named Onund. He was like Yngvar in many ways and most of all in his travels, as referred to in the book called Gesta *Saxonum* which is written as follows: "Fertur, quod Emundus, rex Sveonum, misit filium suum, Onundum, per Mare balzonum, qui, postremo ad amazones veniens, ab eis interfectus est.[13]"

Some men say that Yngvar and his men went for two weeks, that they could not see unless they lit candles, for together the rocks closed over the river, and it was as if they were rowing in a cave that half a month. But wise men do not think it true to be true, unless the river flowed so narrowly that the cliffs met, or the woods were so thick that branches touched together between the cliffs on which they stood. But while this may be so, it is unlikely.

But we have heard this story and written it after the preface of the book that the monk Odd the Learned made at the behest of learned men, whom he himself names in his letter which he sent to Jon Loptsson and Gizur Hallsson. But those who think they know more add it to what is now lacking. This story is said to have been heard by Odd the Monk from a priest named Isleif, and also Glum Thorgeirsson, and Thorir is named as a third source. From their account he took what he found most remarkable. And Isleif said that he had heard

Yngvar's story from a trade, but he said that he had heard it at the court of the King of Sweden. Glum had it from his father, and Thorir had heard it from Klakka Samsson, but Klakka had heard it from his older kinsmen.

And here we close this story.

———————

[1] According to classical authors and medieval bestiaries, the Jaculus was a small, winged dragon that hid in trees and sprang out at its victims like a javelin. Yngvar's Jaculus, however, is much larger.

[2] This town, with its Ancient Greek name meaning 'city of the sun' is imaginary. Perhaps the name was chosen for its exotic, pagan associations.

[3] Evidently not the Red Sea of conventional geography.

[4] A reference to the Byzantine invention called Greek fire, a napalm-like substance whose exact details are lost, although it probably included naphtha, or petroleum.

[5] Not an ethnic term as it is used today: this refers to the Russian river pirates.

[6] This Harald is otherwise unknown to Swedish history and legend.

[7] Soti's bellows?

[8] i.e. 1041 AD

[9] St Olaf, king of Norway.

[10] Constantinople, then capital of the Byzantine Empire.

[11] i.e. the lion.

[12] i.e. the kingdom.

[13] "It is reported that Emundus King of the Swedes sent his son, Onundus, over the Baltic Sea, and finally coming to the Amazons, was killed by them." The Amazons in questions are probably the Kvens, who had a reputation for having women warriors that can be traced back to Tacitus' *Germania*.

Printed in Great Britain
by Amazon